# A NET TO CATCH TIME

BY SARA HARRELL BANKS

ILLUSTRATED BY SCOTT COOK

Alfred A. Knopf · New York

*Never forget the bridge that carries you over.*

*—A Gullah saying*

For Mark and Miss Sara, with love
—S. H. B.

For Jan, whose friendship built a bridge for me
—S. C.

THIS IS A BORZOI BOOK PUBLISHED BY ALFRED A. KNOPF, INC.
Text copyright © 1997 by Sara Harrell Banks
Illustrations copyright © 1997 by Scott Cook

All rights reserved under International and Pan-American Copyright Conventions. Published in the United States by Alfred A. Knopf, Inc., New York, and simultaneously in Canada by Random House of Canada Limited, Toronto. Distributed by Random House, Inc., New York.

http://www.randomhouse.com/

Library of Congress Cataloging-in-Publication Data
Banks, Sara H., 1942–
A net to catch time / by Sara Harrell Banks ; illustrated by Scott Cook.
p. cm.
Summary: Depicts a day in the life of a boy on one of Georgia's barrier islands as sequenced by the Gullah terms for time. Includes an afterword and glossary.
ISBN 0-679-86673-6 (trade) — ISBN 0-679-96673-0 (lib. bdg.)
1. Gullahs—Juvenile fiction. [1. Gullahs—Fiction. 2. Sea Islands—Fiction. 3. Georgia—Fiction. 4. Afro-Americans—Fiction.] I. Cook, Scott, ill. II. Title.
PZ7.B22635Ne    1997    [Fic]—dc20    94-48880

Printed in Singapore
10 9 8 7 6 5 4 3 2 1

# GLOSSARY

**bark**  The shell of a crab.

**bidi-bidi**  A small bird.

**bidy**  Little.

**Bina**  Tuesday. (It is a Gullah custom to name children for the day of their birth.)

**blue**  Believed by the Gullah people to be the color of heaven. (Shutters, doors, and the trim on houses are often painted blue to keep out "haints.")

**conjure**  A spell.

**cooter**  A tortoise.

**croker sack**  A bag woven of hemp or jute. Also called a burlap bag.

**Cuffy**  Friday.

**deviled crabs**  A mixture of cooked crabmeat, onions, herbs, and breadcrumbs stuffed into the "barks," or shells, of crabs. (How good they are depends on the cook!)

**filé**  (fee-LAY) A powder, made from dried sassafras leaves, used for flavoring and as a thickening agent in gumbo.

**frizzled chicken**  This type of chicken looks like it was pulled through a knothole backwards and wet.

**gumbo**  A savory mixture of seafood and vegetables, usually eaten over rice. (The name of the dish comes from the West African word *gombo,* which means "okra.")

**haint**  A ghost.

**hu-hu**  An owl. (Many Gullah words imitate the sound made by the object they describe.)

**okra**  A tall plant with pods, sometimes called "lady's fingers."

*pak*  The sound of knocking.

**plat-eye**  The saucer-shaped eye of a nocturnal animal. (Most have flat eyes, and "plat" means "flat.")

**pot salt**  Coarse salt.

**shisa**  Sister.

**silver dime**  A coin that, when worn, brings good luck. (If the dime tarnishes, someone has cast a spell, or a "conjure," on you.)

**tabby**  A construction material made of burned oyster shells, lime, and sand, mixed with seawater. (Tabby was used by early settlers on Georgia's barrier islands for forts, churches, and houses. The thick, gold-colored walls, scattered through with tiny shells, provided good insulation.)

### Sooner Mornin'
*(about 5:00 a.m.)*
Just before dawn. A lightness on the horizon promises that morning will soon come.

### First Fowl Crow
*(about 5:30 a.m.)*
The rooster crows.

### Day Clean
*(about 6:00 a.m.)*
Dawn breaks, and a fresh, new day begins.

### Hag-Hollerin' Time
*(midnight and after)*
The time, island lore goes, when the wind-driven screams of hags and haints can be heard in the darkness.

# Gullah

### Plat-Eye Prowl
*(between 8:30 p.m. and midnight)*
The night creatures, their eyes flat as plates, awaken from their afternoon sleep and prowl the low country in search of food.

### Black Dark
*(about 8:00 p.m.)*
When you can't see your hand in front of your face.

### Deep Dusk
*(about 7:30 p.m.)*
The evening star shines, ready for wishes.

**Sun-Up**
*(about 6:30 a.m.)*
The people rise with the sun.

**First-Whistle Blow**
*(about 7:30 a.m.)*
In slavery times, a man called a
"driver" blew a conch shell to
call the workers to the fields.

**Noon**
The sun is directly overhead.

# Calendar

**Sun Lay Over**
*(about 2:30 p.m.)*
At mid-afternoon the sun lies
lower in the sky. In the day's
heat, it is nap time for some
and time to lie low for most.

**Candle-Light Time**
*(about 7:00 p.m.)*
Twilight, when the day is
ending and candles glow in the
cabins.

**Sun Down**
*(about 6:30 p.m.)*
The sun falls into the sea.

**Sun Lay Way Over**
*(about 4:30 p.m.)*
The sun slips farther down the
sky and lies way over as the
day begins to cool.

At *SOONER MORNIN'*,

Prince's fishing net

flew through the air

and caught the moon.

Then, gently letting the moon go, it dropped into the silver
moonpath that lay across the water. At last, it dipped into the
sea and caught the little fishes.

Soon, morning would be breaking. Prince was a fisherman,
and it was his custom to fish early while most of the islanders
still slept.

At *FIRST FOWL CROW*, the cabin was wreathed in mist. Cuffy, Prince's son, was fast asleep when the rooster hopped up on the fence post and crowed mightily.

Cuffy opened one eye. Climbing out of bed, he stomped over to the window and threw open the shutters.

"Frizzled ol' bird!" he exclaimed. "You'd make good crab bait. Now hush up before you wake my bidy shisa!"

He looked over his shoulder, not wanting his gran, Dahomey, to hear him. She loved that old rooster, even if it did look like it had been pulled through a knothole backwards and wet.

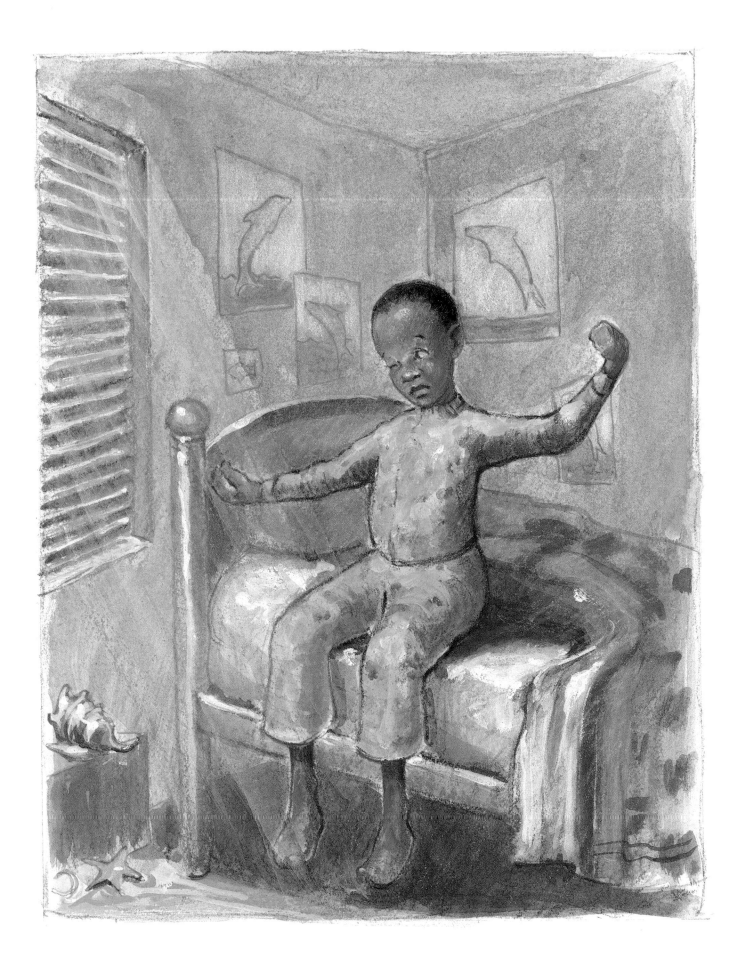

Cuffy washed and dressed quickly. Today he was going crabbing, and he needed an early start.

"Gran, what time?" he called into the kitchen.

"Mornin' to you, too," Dahomey replied. "It's *DAY CLEAN*. Yo' daddy's already gone to the boat." She stood in the doorway, tying her apron around her waist. "But you are *not* goin' to that marsh on an empty stomach. If I know you and your daddy, you'll be workin' from 'til to can't."

At *SUN-UP*, there was a rosy hue over the island. Cuffy watched his gran warm his little sister's bottle. Sitting in her high chair, Bina wore her cereal bowl on her head.

"Hey, bidy shisa," said Cuffy, handing her a slice of his banana. "You look like a cooter wearin' your shell."

Dahomey laughed as Cuffy kissed the baby good-bye. Grabbing his net and croker sack off the front porch, he set out on his way.

Cuffy had a lot to do before he met the ferry boat that came on the afternoon tide. Folks from the mainland loved Dahomey's deviled crabs, and he could sell all she made. But first, he had to catch the crabs for her to cook.

By *FIRST-WHISTLE BLOW,* Cuffy was on his way down the narrow path to the inlet. In the distance, he heard the whistle at the oyster factory, the signal for folks to go to work.

"Time for me to go to work, too," he said to the egret that rose overhead.

The shallows were as clear as sun-washed glass. A crab waved its claw above the water, and Cuffy scooped it up, then dropped it into his sack.

It wasn't long before Cuffy felt his sack getting heavy. He tied it and put it down in the cool shallows just as his daddy rowed in to shore. Cuffy climbed aboard the boat. A line of brown pelicans flew low over the water, and Cuffy counted them. "One...two...three..." There were seven; the uneven number was a good omen.

"That mean we'll find the big blues?" he asked his daddy, pointing to the birds.

"Bound to," said Prince, and together they rowed out to deep water, where the big blue crabs hid.

"I want to catch lots and lots," Cuffy said. "Dahomey said I could keep the money I make sellin' 'em."

"What you gon' do with all that money?" Prince asked.

Cuffy thought for a minute. "Buy me a boat," he said finally. "Then I can be a fisherman, like you."

Prince nodded, pleased. "That would be just fine."

At *NOON,* the sun danced on the water in Dahomey's big black pot. It glittered on the silver dime that she wore on a string around her ankle for good luck. While she waited for the water to boil, she hung the wash out to dry, singing to Bina all the while.

*"New rice and okra, na, na.*

*Eat some and leave some, na, na."*

"Yo' brother needs to be gettin' here," she said, her song over and all the laundry on the line. "Takes time to cook those crabs."

Just then, Prince and Cuffy were pulling their catch into the boat. When all the traps were empty, Prince rowed back to shore. While Prince hung his fishing nets to dry in the hot sun, Cuffy gathered up his crab net and croker sack and walked back home.

At the cabin, Bina lay on a patchwork quilt in the shade of the crepe myrtle tree, looking up at the sky. She smiled when she heard her brother's voice.

"Here, my Dahomey," said Cuffy. "A whole sack full of the fattest crabs you ever saw."

"These are *very* fine!" said Dahomey, spilling the crabs into the pot.

"You a big boy, totin' this all by yo'self." Measuring pot salt into her palm, she added it to the boiling water. Steam rose into the air.

It was *SUN LAY OVER,* the hottest part of the day. The sun's rays dried the marshes, which had drained with the tide, and every little thing lay quiet.

Dahomey slowly stirred the crabmeat mixture in a big blue bowl.

"Close the shutters," she said to Cuffy. "This kitchen gets too hot! And hand me that filé powder, if you please."

High in a pine tree, a woodpecker knocked—*pak . . . pak . . . pak . . .*

"What time is it?" Cuffy asked.

"Time for you to quit pesterin' me," said Dahomey as she filled the crab shells with the delicious mixture. "These be ready soon."

Shadows grew long on the grass. At *SUN LAY WAY OVER,* the sun had slipped farther down in the sky. The day was cooling and the tide turning.

In the distance, the boat whistle blew. The ferry was coming in to the dock! Cuffy ran to get the sign his daddy had printed for him. BEST DEVILED CRABS ON THE ISLAND. MADE BY DAHOMEY LAND. Then he put his empty money jar into his wagon.

"Hurry, my Dahomey," he said. "I have to meet that boat!"

Oyster shells crunched under the tires of Cuffy's wagon. Over the marsh, a blue heron drifted like smoke. A tortoise moved slowly across the path. Cuffy slowed his steps.

"Out the way, little cooter," he said. "I have to meet that boat!"

Cuffy passed the tabby ruins, where the old ones used to live. Something moved. A fawn was gazing at him from the shelter of the trees, the pale spots on its back shining like golden coins.

"Excuse me, little deer," he said. "I have to meet that boat."

The ferry boat was tied up at the dock. The people on board were climbing up the ramp to the shed, where Cuffy waited with his wagon, his sign, and his money jar.

"My Dahomey's deviled crabs are best!" he told everybody.

By *SUN DOWN*, Cuffy had sold all his deviled crabs. When the ferry boat left on the ebb tide, he waved good-bye and put the sign back into his wagon.

Cuffy headed home. With each step he took, the jar of coins jingled in his wagon and his walk grew bouncier. At the tabby ruins, nothing moved now except tiny black frogs hopping across the damp sand.

At *CANDLE-LIGHT TIME*, Prince was inside the cabin, turning the room to gold. The blue front door stood open to catch the breeze. Cuffy left his wagon by the steps and went inside. "Always go in the same door you left by," Dahomey had told him a hundred times. "Don't be bringin' bad luck into this house."

"I hear fine times jinglin'," said Dahomey, smiling at him.

"Was it a good day?" Prince asked.

Bina held out her hands to Cuffy. He poured his coins into the green can, then kissed her palm, which was like a starfish.

"So-so," replied Cuffy, careful not to appear too proud.

At *DEEP DUSK,* the sky darkened. Stars twinkled over the island. Dahomey
began serving up gumbo, rich with okra, tomatoes, and shrimp. Bina smacked
her lips as Prince fed her rice and the juice of the gumbo.

After supper, Dahomey washed the bowls and the teacups, setting them
to dry upside down so the bad luck would run out. Outside the window, a
mockingbird sang.

It was *BLACK DARK* when Cuffy and his daddy sat down together on the front steps of the cabin. An orange moon hung just above the marsh. Bina was in Dahomey's lap, drinking a bottle before bedtime.

Cuffy looked at the moon's reflection on the water. "I wish I could see a whale," he said.

"Someday, maybe," said Prince.

The moon caught in the branches of the live oak tree. From the woods, the little owls—the hu-hus—cried out *hooo...hooo...hooo...*

Dahomey's rocking chair went *creak...creak...creak...*

At *PLAT-EYE PROWL,* the animals with eyes flat as plates prowled for food. Their glowing eyes reflected the moonlight. Bina's head lay heavy against Dahomey's shoulder.

Prince kissed his daughter good night.

"Say good night to yo' shisa," Dahomey told Cuffy softly as she stood to carry the baby inside.

Touching his sister's curls, he whispered, "I'm gon' name my new boat *Bina,* just for you."

In the cabin, Dahomey sang a lullaby to her granddaughter, rocking her gently to sleep.

> *"Ferry boat gon' carry us over,*
> *The robe all ready now.*
> *Ferry boat gon' carry us over,*
> *The robe all ready now."*

Cuffy grew sleepy. He leaned his head against his daddy's knee. From the heavens, a star fell into the sea.

"Take my hand," said Prince. Then Cuffy and his daddy closed the blue door against the night.

Stories were told on the island about *HAG-HOLLERIN' TIME,* about haints and hags screaming in the darkness. But as midnight approached, only the cries of screech owls split the silence. The full moon spilled into the room where Cuffy and his daddy were sleeping. In his dream, Cuffy rode on a dolphin's back to see the great whales. Dahomey slept next to Bina. Bina was awake in the dark, listening to the call of the hu-hus.

At *SOONER MORNIN',*

Prince's fishing net

flew through the air

and caught the moon.

# AUTHOR'S NOTE

Several years ago, while visiting one of Georgia's barrier islands, I was given an oddly beautiful calendar by a man who was Gullah. "Since you're a writer," he said, "you might want to save it." Like a book of hours that measured time in words, it was less a calendar than a Gullah timepiece. And save it I did. For a long time, it was tucked away among my papers, those bits and pieces that writers gather and hoard. I'd take it out and read it from time to time, savoring its sounds but not sure just how to use it.

When I came back home to Savannah, one of the things I discovered was that the Gullah communities that I had taken for granted were disappearing. Commercial development and attrition were destroying the Gullah culture that had once stretched from Savannah to St. Mary's. I remembered my calendar, read it once again, and decided to write this book.

Cuffy's island could be one of several where, in the 1800s, African slaves were brought to work the great rice plantations. On these islands, the customs and superstitions of half a hundred tribes mingled to form a unique way of life. Here, in isolation, the Gullah culture was born.

The lyrical language, with its lilting cadences that describe an island's beauty as "de God wok," grows fainter, more distant. The Gullah calendar reflects the simple eloquence of a language and a way of life that is, indeed, something to "save." It is candle-light time. The day grows short.